4 November 2017

The Bright Red Mark

Dear Reader,

I hope you enjoy this quiet and gentle story as you journey along with our lovely Keiko!

Keep reading,

J. F. CIOFALO

J. F. Cio[illegible]

Archway Publishing books may be ordered through booksellers or by contacting:

Archway Publishing
1663 Liberty Drive
Bloomington, IN 47403
www.archwaypublishing.com
1 (888) 242-5904

ISBN: 978-1-4808-3917-5 (sc)
ISBN: 978-1-4808-3918-2 (hc)
ISBN: 978-1-4808-3916-8 (e)

Print information available on the last page.

Archway Publishing rev. date: 11/29/2016

When Keiko was born, she looked splendid – except for one thing: a bright red mark adorned her right cheek. No, it was not large and it certainly did not hurt, but still the people all stared at Keiko with great curiosity. Her mother just smiled and hugged her tightly with her soft, warm arms.

One day when Keiko was two years old, she looked at herself in a clear pool and pointed to the bright red mark on her cheek.

“It’s a sign, Keiko,” explained her mother. “A drop of paint from the brush of some great artist has splashed on your face. It means that someday you too will become a great artist.”

As Keiko grew older, she felt quite proud of her bright red mark because she understood what it meant. She looked forward to the day when she would be known to everyone as a great artist. Keiko wished to share this joy and excitement with the world, so she ran outside to tell her friends.

“Someday I am going to be a great artist, you know,” she told the bright Moon high up in the sky.

“How marvelous!” answered the Moon. “What will you think?”

“I shall think noble thoughts and use all the colors of the rainbow to bring them to life,” said Keiko.

She also chatted with the stately Tree which stood high upon a large hill.

"Tree," said Keiko, "I am going to be a great artist when I grow up."

"That's terrific!" responded the Tree. "What will you do?"

"I shall paint beautiful pictures that will make all the people happy," said Keiko.

She even held a conversation with the frosty Snow as it drifted down from the grey sky.

"Did you hear, Snow?" asked Keiko. "I shall be a great artist some day."

"Oh, sensational!" replied the Snow. "What will you feel?"

"I shall feel a great sense of worthiness and much dignity," said Keiko.

In the autumn of her life, Keiko's mother became very ill. She lay in bed and watched the brilliant colors fade into winter.

"Do not forget, Daughter," she said touching her bright red mark, "you must learn to be a great artist someday."

Then she hugged little Keiko tightly between her warm arms and closed her eyes.

Now Keiko was alone in the world except for her friends. At nighttime, the Moon would sing soft lullabys to put her to sleep. And when the wind blew, the Tree would sway to and fro and whisper wonderful secrets to the girl. On cold winter nights, the Snow would sigh as it gently fell to earth making a warm blanket for her. Keiko grew to admire and respect her friends a great deal.

One delightful spring day Keiko announced that it was time for her to become a great artist.

“I’m going to learn how to paint today,” she told the Tree. “I shall think a noble thought and create a beautiful picture. Then everyone will be happy.”

But Keiko discovered that no matter what she thought about, the colors only dribbled and smeared on the paper. Though she tried many times, she simply could not paint a picture that would make anyone happy. Keiko felt anger and sadness in her heart.

“Now I shall never become a great artist,” she complained to her friends. “My mother has lied to me about the bright red mark.”

“Perhaps you need to think some more,” said the Moon.

“Perhaps you have not done enough,” offered the Tree.

“Perhaps you ought to feel differently,” suggested the Snow.

But Keiko did not listen. She felt too sorry for herself to hear their words. Slowly, the bright red mark began to fade from her cheek until it was nearly gone.

One evening as it rocked up the mountaintop, the Moon said, “Keiko, we still respect you, you know.”

“You do?” asked Keiko with great surprise. “Even though I cannot paint beautiful pictures?”

“Of course,” replied the Moon. “Come be our friend again and we shall teach you to be wise and happy.”

And so Keiko did. She romped through green meadows with the Moon and laughed each month as its face grew round and chubby.

She swung from the Tree's strong branches
and lay in its shade on hot, summer days.

In winter, she caught the white Snow in her hands
and marveled at each lovely flake.

Together, Keiko and her friends shared many wonderful times, and soon the days blended into years. Keiko had indeed become a wise and happy woman.

Late one afternoon as Keiko rested under the Tree, a young woman visited her.

“I have come to thank you for my life.” said the woman.

“What do you mean?” asked Keiko, very surprised.

“For several years,” explained the woman, “I have watched you speak to the Moon, dance beneath the Tree, and frolic in the Snow. You have painted such a beautiful picture for me and that is how I wish to live my life. Truly you are a great artist.”

Keiko just smiled and felt much worthiness and dignity inside.

That night as the Moon sang a soft lullaby, it noticed a big smile on Keiko's face and a bright red mark on her cheek.

The End

Edwards Brothers Malloy
Thorofare, NJ USA
January 19, 2017